BUNNY RACE!

To Ken — G.M.

For Kara and Neil — E.L.

Text copyright © 2009 by Grace Maccarone.
Illustrations copyright © 2009 by The Ethan Long Studio, Inc.

Library of Congress Cataloging-in-Publication Data
Maccarone, Grace.
Bunny race / by Grace Maccarone ; illustrated by Ethan Long.
p. cm.
"Cartwheel books."
Summary: Four rabbits compete in a race using different
means of transportation.
ISBN-10: 0-545-11250-8 (pbk.)
ISBN-13: 978-0-545-11250-5 (pbk.)
ISBN-10: 0-545-11290-7 (hardcover)
ISBN-13: 978-0-545-11290-1 (hardcover)
[1. Stories in rhyme. 2.Racing–Fiction.
3. Rabbits–Fiction. 4. Transportation–Fiction.]
I.Long, Ethan, ill. II. Title.
PZ8.3.M127Bun 2009
[E]–dc22   2008022454

ISBN-13: 978-0-545-11250-5
ISBN-10: 0-545-11250-8

10 9 8 7 6 5 4 3   40   10 11 12 13/0

Printed in the U.S.A.
First printing, January 2009

BUNNY RACE!

by Grace Maccarone
Illustrated by Ethan Long

Cartwheel
·B·O·O·K·S·®

SCHOLASTIC INC.
New York Toronto London Auckland Sydney
Mexico City New Delhi Hong Kong Buenos Aires

The bunny race
will now begin.

Can you guess
which one will win?

Chapter 1: Driver Bunny

Bunny has
a little car.

It can go fast.
It can go far.

It can go up.

It can go down.

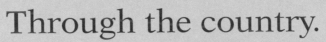

Through the country.

Through the town.

It goes so fast.
It's off the track.

That's not the way.
Come back! Come back!

Chapter 2: Sailor Bunny

Bunny has
a little boat.

See it glide.
See it float.

See it sink.
Oh, no, no, no.
The bunny boat
goes down below.

Swordfish, tunas,
crabs, and whales

play hide-and-seek
among the sails.

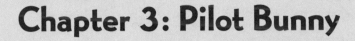

Chapter 3: Pilot Bunny

Bunny has
a big balloon.
See it fly
up to the moon.

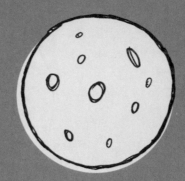

Past the planets.

Past a star.
The big balloon
has gone too far.

Up and up
and up it goes.
Will it come back?
No bunny knows.

Chapter 4: Runner Bunny

Bunny has
two bunny feet.
They are fast.
And they are fleet.

They can run.

And they can hop.

They can go.

And they can stop.

They take her here.

They take her there.

Her two feet take
her everywhere.

They take her
to the finish line.

Her bunny feet
have worked just fine.

All the bunnies come back now.
And Runner Bunny takes a bow.